D0385232

Bill Buffalo

Dave and Pat Sargent are longtime residents of Prairie Grove, Arkansas. Dave, a fourth-generation dairy farmer, began writing in early December 1990, and Pat, a former teacher, began writing shortly after. They enjoy the outdoors and have a real love for animals.

Bill Buffalo

By

Dave and Pat Sargent

Illustrated by
Jeane Huff

Ozark Publishing, Inc.
P.O. Box 228
Prairie Grove, AR 72753

Library of Congress cataloging-in-publication data

Sargent, Dave, 1941—
    Bill Buffalo / by Dave and Pat Sargent ; illustrated
by Jeane Huff.
    p. cm.
    Summary: Teased by the other buffaloes because his
hair is black instead of brown, Bill Buffalo finally
learns to accept himself for what he really is.
    ISBN 1-56763-360-9 (cb). — ISBN 1-56763-
361-7 (pb)
    [1. Bison—Fiction.   2. Self-acceptance—
    Fiction.]
    I. Sargent, Pat, 1936—   .
    II. Huff, Jeane, 1946—
    ill.   III. Title.
    PZ7.S2465Bg   1998
    97-27199
    [E]—dc21
                                                    CIP
                                                    AC

Printed in the United States of America

iv

Inspired by

our love of animals and the wide open spaces.

Dedicated to

our granddaughter April.

Foreword

Little Bill Buffalo is different. The other young buffalo make fun of him because he is a different color. He learns that it's not the color you are that's important. It's what's inside you that counts.

Contents

Bill Buffalo

If you would like to have the authors of the Animal Pride Series visit your school, free of charge, call 1-800-321-5671 or 1-800-960-3876.

One

A New Black Calf

It was late winter, and the large buffalo herd was looking for a place out of the cold wind to bed down for the night. All the cows were due to start calving just any day now.

The buffalo knew they would have to find refuge from the wind. They roamed the prairie, searching for such a place. Finally, they found a large creek with a steep, high bank on the north side. This would do fine. It would give them protection from the cold night air. The herd

1

bedded down for the night in the shelter of the high bank.

Fada, one of the young buffalo cows, was feeling poorly. Early that morning, her stomach had started hurting, and she knew it was time for her calf to be born.

Poor Fada was having a rough time of it. She would lay on one side for a while, then would get up and lay on the other side. She was miserable all night long. Finally, around four o'clock in the morning, she gave birth to a baby calf, a boy. By the time the sun came up, the new baby calf was on his feet and nursing.

When it got light enough to see well, Fada noticed something really strange about her new baby. Her brand-new baby calf was solid black. He was as black as the ace of spades. He didn't have a brown spot on him.

Fada noticed the other cows craning their necks in her direction. She saw them coming closer and closer, eying her new baby. They had never seen a black buffalo calf before either. Fada didn't know whether to be happy or sad because her baby was different.

The little black calf didn't care what color he was or that everyone was staring at him. He went about his business. His business was, quite simply, nursing and sleeping.

One day, Fada looked down at her baby and asked, "What are we going to call you, little boy?"

The little black buffalo didn't answer. He just looked at his mama.

"Let's see. How about Bill? Do you like the name Bill?" she asked.

The little buffalo was too busy to answer. He was a little over three months old now and had just started eating grass. Eating grass was fun!

He just loved getting the tender green blades of grass in his mouth and biting them off with his teeth. He always gave his head a little jerk when he bit off a mouthful of grass.

Bill was having such fun eating. He was so busy eating that he wasn't paying a bit of attention to what his mama was asking him.

"Bill! That is your name. Bill! I'm going to call you Bill Buffalo." Mama Buffalo had pondered this name thing for three long months, and she seemed relieved that she had finally picked a name for her son.

Two

Buffalo Are Brown

The buffalo cows and their new babies were always grazing close to Bill and his mama. Recently, Bill had begun noticing how all the other calves stared and laughed at him.

The little calves were beginning to hurt Bill's feelings. He just couldn't understand why the others treated him like they did. Why, sometimes, late at night, he cried.

One day, while the buffalo were roaming, Bill decided to ask one of the calves why they teased him so.

Bill worked his way over to Bobby. He took a deep breath and asked, "Bobby, why do you and the other calves tease me so much? And why don't you guys want me around you? You and your friends don't ever play with me, and when I start toward you, all of you run away from me. Why do you guys do that? Don't you like me? Huh? Is that it? You don't like me?"

13

Bobby had begun laughing when Bill started talking, and now, Bobby laughed even harder as he answered, "Why should we like you when you don't even look like us? You are really weird looking, Bill! You are black. Buffalo are brown. You don't even look like a buffalo!"

That did it! Bill ran back to his mama, but this time, he didn't cry. He was mad. Bill was mad because he was different. And all this time, he had thought he was a buffalo, just like his mama.

Mama Buffalo was very tired. Mama Buffalo and the entire buffalo herd had been on the move since early dawn. In the summertime, there were more daylight hours, so during the summer, the herd spent more time roaming.

When Mama Buffalo saw Bill coming toward her, she stopped. She knew something was wrong. Since Bill's face looked so mad, she figured the other calves had been teasing him again. He was stomping his feet and slinging his head from side to side.

"What is it, Bill? What's wrong with you?" Mama Buffalo asked.

"Nothing. Nothing is wrong, Mama," Bill answered as he fell into step beside her.

"Are they still teasing you about your color, Bill? Is that it?" Mama Buffalo asked. "Are they teasing you because you are not brown like the rest of us?"

Bill looked the other way. He did not want to talk about the others. He did not want to tattle on them, even though they had made fun of him. He thought it was wrong to tattle.

"It's okay, Bill," Mama said. "You can tell me."

Bill took a deep breath before he asked, "Why am I black, Mama? Why am I black, when you and all the other calves and their mamas are

17

brown? What's wrong with me, Mama? What is it? Please tell me. Why am I a different color?"

Mama Buffalo smiled at Bill. "I don't know, Bill. I really don't know why you are a different color. But when you shed your summer hair, maybe the black will be gone. When your new winter coat comes in, you will look like the rest of us. You will not always be black, Bill. Just wait a little longer. You'll see."

That seemed to satisfy Bill at least for the present. He went about his business of grazing and roaming alongside his mama.

Bill watched the other calves. As they grazed, they laughed at him. For the most part, Bill ignored them, or tried to. But it was really hard, pretending not to see them when they were making such fun of him.

Remembering what his mama had said about his new winter coat being a different color made it much easier for Bill to get through the days ahead.

Bill got all excited when he first noticed his black hair falling out. It was even more noticeable when he accidentally brushed against his mama or one of the other buffalo.

Looking around, he saw the same thing happening to the other calves and their mamas. It wouldn't be long now until he looked like the others. Boy! He could hardly wait!

Three

A Magnificent Red Coat

The weather was definitely changing. The days were getting cooler, and Bill and the other buffalo were now getting thick winter coats. Bill was always looking over his shoulder, trying to see if his back was turning brown. But the hair on his back wasn't turning brown. His front legs were not brown, either. Bill could not believe his eyes! No! Oh, no! His legs were turning red!

"Mama! Mama!" Bill called. "Look, Mama! Look at my legs!"

Bill's mama had been dreading this day. She had been dreading the day Bill noticed that he had red hair. When it came to Bill's red hair, she was completely buffaloed, as the saying goes. This meant that she did not know what to think about Bill's red legs and back and neck and head, and of course, Bill's long, red tail! Why, his entire body was covered with thick, red hair!

"You are not the same color as the rest of us, Bill, but that's okay. You don't really *have* to be brown. Nowhere is it written that buffalo have to be brown. I suppose buffalo can be any color," Mama Buffalo said. "You see, Bill, it's not the color you are that's important. It's what's inside you that counts. It's what you feel in your heart."

Bill was trying to listen to what his mama was saying. But it was hard to do. He could feel and hear the other calves and their mamas laughing and making fun of him.

Bill asked, "What can I do to make them stop making fun of me, Mama?"

Mama thought for a minute, then said, "Well, now, let me see. Perhaps if you work hard and try to be the best at everything you do, they will notice you because you are a good worker. I think that would help. Don't you?"

After Bill thought it over, he agreed with his mama. He decided to try hard to make the others notice him and accept him.

Bill started helping the old and sickly buffalo whenever he could. He started exercising a lot, and soon, Bill developed big, bulging muscles.

Bill started growing. He grew both in stature and in the eyes of the young buffalo.

All the buffalo, both young and old, began noticing Bill. They saw his bulging muscles, his bright eyes, and his pretty, shiny coat. And soon they forgot that Bill was different. They even forgot about Bill having red hair.

Everyone saw Bill Buffalo for what he really was. Bill had become a very caring, very dedicated worker. He was an asset to the buffalo herd. And soon it occurred to Bill's mama that Bill, her little red-haired buffalo, was destined to be a great leader. Yes, Bill was a natural-born leader.

The buffalo herd roamed all over the plains. After Bill worked hard at being the best he could be, one day, when he was full grown, Bill roamed at the front of the herd. The herd now accepted him as their leader.

This was a great time for Bill. He had worked hard and had done his best. He had turned his problem into something good.

Bill's beautiful red coat was easy to spot. And when new calves were born every July, as soon as they were old enough to ask, "Who is our leader, Mama?" Mama would point to Bill and reply, "Do you see the big bull at the front of our herd? He is our leader. His name is Bill Buffalo. He is the one with the magnificent red coat."

BILL BUFFALO
GREAT BUFFALO LEADER

Four

Buffalo Facts

A bison is either of two existing species of the wild cattle genus Bison. One, commonly but incorrectly known as the buffalo, is the American bison. The other, the European species, is the wisent.

A bull of the American buffalo, or bison, may weigh around two thousand pounds and stand more than six feet high. The massive head and forequarters are covered with long hair, and the body slims down toward the hindquarters, which are covered with shorter hair. The female of the species is somewhat smaller. Both sexes have horns, but those of the male are more massive. A single calf is born after a gestation period of nine months.

The bison was a principal resource of the Plains Indians, furnishing them with food, skins for shelter and boats, bones for tools and utensils, and "buffalo chips" (dung) for fuel.

shields food

fuel

tools

shelter

blankets   moccasins

Few wild animals have under-gone a more devastating encounter with humans than the bison. The grasslands from the Mississippi River to the Rocky Mountains were the home of thirty million bison when white settlers first arrived. These numbers were reduced to five hundred near the end of the last century, and then slowly increased to an estimated thirty-five to fifty thousand on refuges and ranches today.

The European bison, or the Bison bonasus, known as the wisent, may weigh twenty-two hundred pounds and stand more than six feet one inch high. In comparison with the American bison, the wisent has longer legs and a smaller head with longer horns. Lacking the shaggy coat of the American bison, the wisent appears more ox-like.

The wisent inhabits woodlands and feeds on grasses, ferns, leaves, and tree bark. At one time the wisent ranged from western Europe to Siberia. The destruction of the forests led to the decline of the bison population in Europe. The wisent is no longer endangered.